Usborne ~~B~~

Trucks

Katie Daynes
Designed by Zoe Wray

Illustrations by Christyan Fox

Truck consultant: David Riley

Reading consultant: Alison Kelly
Roehampton University of Surrey

Contents

Truck travel

Trucks carry all kinds of things from one place to another.

The things a truck carries are called its load.

Trucks and trailers

Some trucks come in two parts. The trailer is where the load is kept and the cab is where the driver sits.

Trailer

Cab

Wires and tubes carry electricity and air to the trailer. These make the back lights and brakes work.

The trailer rests on two landing legs.

The cab backs up to meet the trailer.

They join together and drive away.

When trailer trucks reach a bend, the cab turns first, then the trailer follows.

A cab can join up with different shapes of trailers.

5

Truck bodies

Not all trucks have two parts. On many trucks the trailer is attached to the cab.

This truck is taking fresh bananas to a market

Some very small trucks only have three wheels.

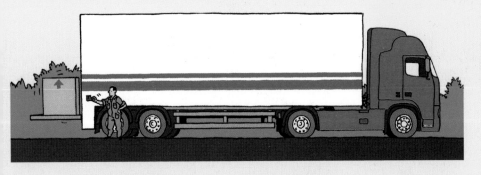

Box body trucks have hard sides and open up at the back.

Soft-sided trucks have sides that open like a big curtain.

On flatbed trucks, the load lies flat on the trailer and is tied down with rope.

Loading up

Lots of trucks collect their loads from huge buildings called warehouses.

A forklift truck picks up a crate on a pallet.

It takes it outside and lifts it up onto a truck.

The crates are stacked inside the truck.

Some loads, such as racehorses, can walk onto their trucks.

This truck has its own crane. The driver is using it to load up.

On the road

Often trucks have to take their load to somewhere far away.

The journey may take several days.

Many countries make drivers take a break during the day so they don't get too tired.

Truck drivers take breaks at truck stops.

On long journeys they can rest, eat and sleep in their trucks.

Inside the cab there is room to relax.

A bed folds down from the wall.

11

Across the sea

Trucks may have to take their loads across the sea on a ferry.

Trucks arrive at a port. They drive up a ramp, onto a ferry.

The ferry closes its back door and sets sail across the sea.

When it reaches land, the front of the ferry opens and the trucks drive off.

Some loads are lifted onto a ship, leaving the truck behind.

The ship crosses the sea and the load is put on another truck.

The load travels inside a box called a container. Cranes lift the containers on and off the ship.

Container crane

Containers

Tanker trucks

Tanker trucks carry liquids or gases in big tanks on their trailers.

Milk tankers collect milk from farms. The milk goes through a pipe into the tank.

Cows are milked twice a day. The tanker collects the milk on the same day.

Fuel tankers take
fuel to gas stations.

At the gas station,
pipes are attached
to the tanker.

The fuel goes from
the tanker into big
tanks under the ground.

Fuel
tank

Fuel
tank

Dump trucks

Dump trucks are huge trucks that carry sand, dirt and chunks of rock.

The driver has to climb up some steps to reach the cab.

A big digger fills the truck with scoops of dirt.

The truck takes the dirt away, then dumps it out.

Some dump trucks have wheels taller than two tall men.

17

Fire trucks

Fire trucks bring firefighters, ladders and water to places where there's a fire.

The firefighters open up the side to reach their equipment.

They unwind hoses and attach them to the truck's water tank.

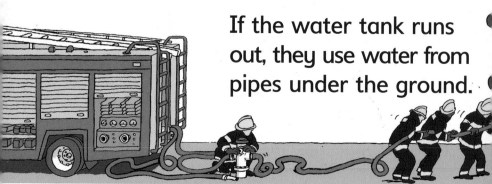

If the water tank runs out, they use water from pipes under the ground.

Ladders stretch up from the back of the trucks and firefighters spray water on the fire.

Some fire trucks have platforms that reach up to rescue people.

Heavy loads

Trucks that carry big, heavy loads have many wheels or move on tracks.

This transporter truck is carrying a space shuttle. Can you see the truck cab?

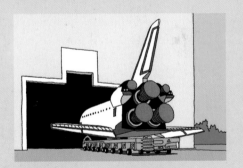

The transporter takes the shuttle into a warehouse.

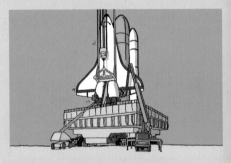

Cranes help lift the shuttle onto a crawler truck.

Space shuttle

The crawler has tracks instead of wheels. It carries the shuttle to its launch pad.

Track

The shuttle crawler travels even slower than a person walking.

Dirty work

Trashmen collect trash and carry it away in trash trucks.

A dumpster is hooked onto the truck. It is lifted up and the trash is tipped out.

A big metal plate squashes down the trash to make more room.

To empty the truck, the end lifts up and a metal plate pushes the trash out.

A bigger truck takes the trash to a place where it can be burned or buried.

Some trash can be used again. This dump truck is delivering plastic bags to a recycling plant.

Hot and cold

Around the world, trucks are shaped differently to suit the jobs they do.

Road trains are big trucks with several trailer

They travel long distances on very straight roads. Some drive all the way across deserts

Road trains meet very little traffic so they can travel quickly.

In snowy mountains,
trucks are used to flatten
the snow on the ski slopes.

They have tracks instead of wheels to keep
them from slipping on the snow.

The front of the
truck scoops snow
out of the way.

At the back there
are brushes to
smooth the snow.

25

Car transporters

Car transporters carry cars to garages.
Follow the numbers to see how they load up

Deck

1. A car reverses onto a deck and is tipped up

2. Two cars follow, then that deck is raised.

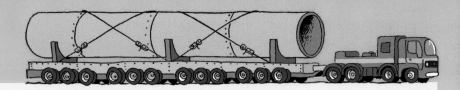

Some trucks have more than 50 wheels.

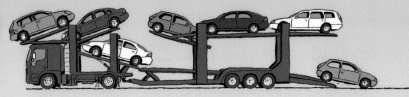

3. Three cars drive onto a deck above the cab.

4. Six more cars fit onto other decks below.

Truck sports

Some trucks don't carry loads. Instead they take part in truck sports.

These trucks are having a race.
They drive around a track at high speed.

Some very fast trucks have jet engines, just like planes.

Once a year there is a truck race that goes across the Sahara desert and takes 21 days.

Monster trucks take part in jumping competitions.

The monster truck speeds up a ramp.

It jumps up and over a big object.

Then it lands with a bump on the ground.

Glossary of truck words

Here are some of the words in this book you might not know. This page tells you what they mean.

 load - the things carried by a truck.

 cab - the front part of a truck where the truck driver sits.

 trailer - a load carrier on wheels that is pulled by a truck.

 pallet - a big tray used in warehouses. Forklift trucks lift up crates on pallets.

 truck stop - like a parking lot, but for trucks. Drivers can stay the night here

 ferry - a boat that takes people, trucks and cars across the sea.

 recycling - making new objects from old objects that are collected by trucks

Web sites to visit

If you have a computer, you can find out more about trucks on the Internet. On the Usborne Quicklinks Web site there are links to four fun Web sites.

Web site 1 - Make different trucks with the three cards on your screen.

Web site 2 - Find out more about dump trucks and building sites.

Web site 3 - See photos of trucks from around the world.

Web site 4 - Learn what each part of a fire truck does.

To visit these Web sites, go to **www.usborne-quicklinks.com** and type the keywords "beginners trucks". Then click on the link for the Web site you want to visit. Before you use the Internet, look at the safety guidelines inside the back cover of this book and ask an adult to read them with you.

Index

Acknowledgements

Managing editor: Fiona Watt, Managing designer: Mary Cartwright
Photographic manipulation by Emma Julings and John Russell
American editor: Carrie Seay

Photo credits

The publishers are grateful to the following for permission to reproduce material:
© **Alvey & Towers** Cover, 1, 5, 28, © **Bill Noonan, Boston Fire Department** 19,
© **Corbis** (Kevin R. Morris) 6, (Joseph Sohm; ChromoSohm Inc.) 9, (Ted Spiegel) 11,
(Richard Hamilton Smith) 16-17, (Richard T. Nowitz) 23, (Christine Osborne) 24,
© **The Dairy Council** 14, © **Digital Vision** 4, 10, 12-13, 16-17, 23, 24, © **ECM (Vehicle
Delivery Service) Ltd** 26-27, © **Kässbohrer Geländefahrzeug AG** (PistenBully) 25,
© **Malcolm Birks** 31, © **NASA** 20, 21, © **Nissan/dppi** 29, © **Volvo Truck Limited** 2-3, 15

With thanks to

Henry Brook, Chris Hodge Trucks (www.chrishodgetrucks.co.uk),
Bill Noonan, Steven Askew, Wolfgang Lutz and The Dairy Council

First published in 2002 by Usborne Publishing Ltd., Usborne House, 83-85 Saffron Hill, London EC1N 8RT,
England. www.usborne.com Copyright © 2002 Usborne Publishing Ltd. The name Usborne and the devices ♀ ⊕
are Trade Marks of Usborne Publishing Ltd. All rights reserved. No part of this publication may be reproduced,
stored in a retrieval system, or transmitted in any form or by any means, electronic, mechanical,
photocopying, recording or otherwise, without the prior permission of the publisher.
First published in America 2003. A.E. Printed in Belgium.

Internet safety rules

- Ask your parent's or guardian's permission before you connect to the Internet.

- When you are on the Internet, never tell anyone your full name, address or telephone number, and ask an adult before you give your e-mail address.

- If a Web site asks you to log in or register by typing your name or e-mail address, ask an adult's permission first.

- If you do receive an e-mail from someone you don't know, tell an adult and do not reply to the e-mail.

Notes for parents or guardians

The Web sites described in this book are regularly reviewed and the links in Usborne Quicklinks are updated. However, the content of a Web site may change at any time and Usborne Publishing is not responsible, and does not accept liability, for the content or availability of any Web site other than its own, or for any exposure to harmful, offensive or inaccurate material which may appear on the Web. We recommend that children are supervised while on the Internet, that they do not use Internet Chat Rooms and that you use Internet filtering software to block unsuitable material. Please ensure that your children follow the safety guidelines printed above. For more information, see the "Net Help" area on the Usborne Quicklinks Web site at **www.usborne-quicklinks.com**

Usborne Beginners

Trucks

There are lots of different trucks – crawler trucks, road trains, flatbed trucks, monster trucks, fire trucks and many more. Find out what they all do and how they work in this fascinating book.

Trucks is part of an exciting new series of books for children who are beginning to read on their own. The easy-to-read text has been specially written with the help of a reading expert.

Other titles in this series:
Bears, Castles, Caterpillars and butterflies, Eggs and chicks, How flowers grow, Living in space, Night animals, Planes, Spiders, Tadpoles and frogs, Under the sea

For more information about Usborne Publishing, visit **www.edcpub.com** or **www.ubah.com**

Published in the USA by
EDC PUBLISHING, 10302 E. 55th Place,
Tulsa, Oklahoma 74146, USA.

NOT FOR SALE IN CANADA

$4.95
0-7945-0365-9
JFMAMJJASO D/03

Made with paper from a sustainable forest.

Candlewick Sparks offer newly independent readers the chance to experience early fiction from some of today's most talented authors and illustrators. Endearing and enduring, these extraordinary books are guaranteed to ignite the imagination.

Praise for *Joe and Sparky Get New Wheels*

★ "Children . . . will laugh out loud at the innocent assumptions Joe . . . and Sparky make as they explore the world outside Sparky's shell. Utterly charming." —*Kirkus Reviews* (starred review)

"A silly, action-packed tale for fluent early readers." —*School Library Journal*

"Sure to keep readers laughing." —*Children's Literature*

✦ ✦ ✦

Jamie Michalak is a children's book editor and writer. About this book, she says, "My sister, Julie, inspired this story. Like Joe and Sparky, she and I had many adventures together. Adventure is around every corner—you just have to stretch your neck and look for it." Jamie Michalak lives in Barrington, Rhode Island, with her husband and two sons. She does not have super driving skills.

Frank Remkiewicz has illustrated many books for children. Among them are the Piggy and Dad Brand New Readers and the picture book *Piggy and Dad Go Fishing,* all written by David Martin. About watching his books being read to children, the artist says, "I like it when they smile, but I love it when they laugh." He lives on the Gulf Coast of Florida.